Louie's little LEGS

and the Magic of PATIENCE

Danise DiStasi and Mea Sobb
with Evi Sobb

Illustrated by Rachel Royer

Copyright © 2021 by Danise DiStasi, Loveland, OH

All rights reserved.

ISBN: 978-1-7327067-4-3 (hard cover)
ISBN: 978-1-7327067-5-0 (soft cover)

Library of Congress Control Number: 2021917655

Danise DiStasi and Mea Sobb
Creative Assistant: Evi Sobb
Book Editor: Ashley Williams
Cover and Book Illustrator: Rachel Royer
Interior Typesetting: Lori Weidert

Visit our site: unleash-love.com

My eyes opened wide as I greeted the new dawn!
"Good morning, little Louie," Amee said as she yawned.

Her eyes were still closed, and her voice slowly faded.
She drifted back to sleep as I lay awake and waited.

Amee slooooooowly stretched, and I started to wiggle.
She loved me and cuddled me, and my legs that are little.

Amee fixed my food as I sat still and watched.
She ate her pancakes
while the minutes clicked by on the clock.

Finally, we raced out the door, and we jumped, and we leaped.
My legs might be little, but they run with such speed.

We ran down the street and beyond the school zone
to the next block over— to our friend Jackie's home.

Jackie was waiting, and the friends laughed and hugged.
I panted and smiled, being such a patient pup.
"Where to today, little Louie?" the friends asked as they smiled.
"Let's go to the fair and play games for a while!"

Surprise!

It's my friend Rascal, and he settled down before us.
He's so fluffy and fast.
When he runs, he turns into a puff!

"Did someone say the fair?" he asked rather quickly.
Rascal is a rascally puppy who's so fun and so silly.

He ran and he ran in circles all around me,
'til he soon disappeared in a puff with such glee.

"Let's go," Rascal laughed as he pulled me to the sky.
Our mouths opened wide and we started to fly.

Our fluffy puff soared past the birds and the trees,
past the other big clouds whisked away by the breeze.

We drifted down slowly 'til we touched the green grass.
We were at the fairgrounds, where we wanted to be, at last.

My little legs stopped as I noticed a dog
who took one step forward with his big, heavy paws.

"Who do you think you are?"

His loud voice was so gruff.
But that didn't keep Rascal from running straight toward the truck.

My little legs walked right up to the toughie.
"Now, that's not very nice.
Can't you see he's a puppy?"

"I don't care about that.
I know his kind. He thinks since he's cute
he can step in front of the line.
Well, that won't work with me.
I've been waiting too long. Go back to the end
before I do something wrong."

Rascal's lip began to quiver, and he started to cry.
"Don't worry, Rascal. Let's go to the end of the line."
"But, but," Rascal said.
"I can hardly wait!
There are rides and games and, oh, the raspberry cake!"

His eyes grew wider and wider, and he started to huff.

His paws lifted off the ground in a moment of fluff.

"Rascal," I said as I pulled on his paw, "don't let this upset you.

We can patiently wait and still have fun too!"

"No matter what someone says, we must be patient and kind. There's a magical secret to patience you'll learn in due time."

Rascal's face lit up as he sat unbelievably still. "Tell me the secret, and I'll learn it—I will!"

"The secret to being patient," I said with a wink, "is to do one thing at a time! PAWS... and just do the very next thing."

ICE CREAM

"You'll learn to be patient by doing the next thing.
Don't run ahead of yourself or try to do everything!
That's the magic of patience, taking one moment at a time.
Focus on what's in front of you; don't rush ahead, especially in line."

"I guess you're right. I didn't mean to offend.
I should do the next thing — I should go to the end."
Our little legs took us to the end of the line.
We made new friends while we waited. Even Spike was more kind.

After eating our cones, we laughed and we played.
Then I stopped and asked Rascal, "What's the next thing to do today?"

"Oh, the rides and games and the Ferris wheel."

And his eyes grew wide in his moment of zeal.

He started to pant and then began to rise.
"But maybe for now, we should stand in line for the rides."

Our fun day had ended. The bright stars twinkled above.
While we walked home together, I pondered my favorite word, love.

Love is being patient and kind, no matter how tough.
We should just do the next thing,
one step at a time is enough.

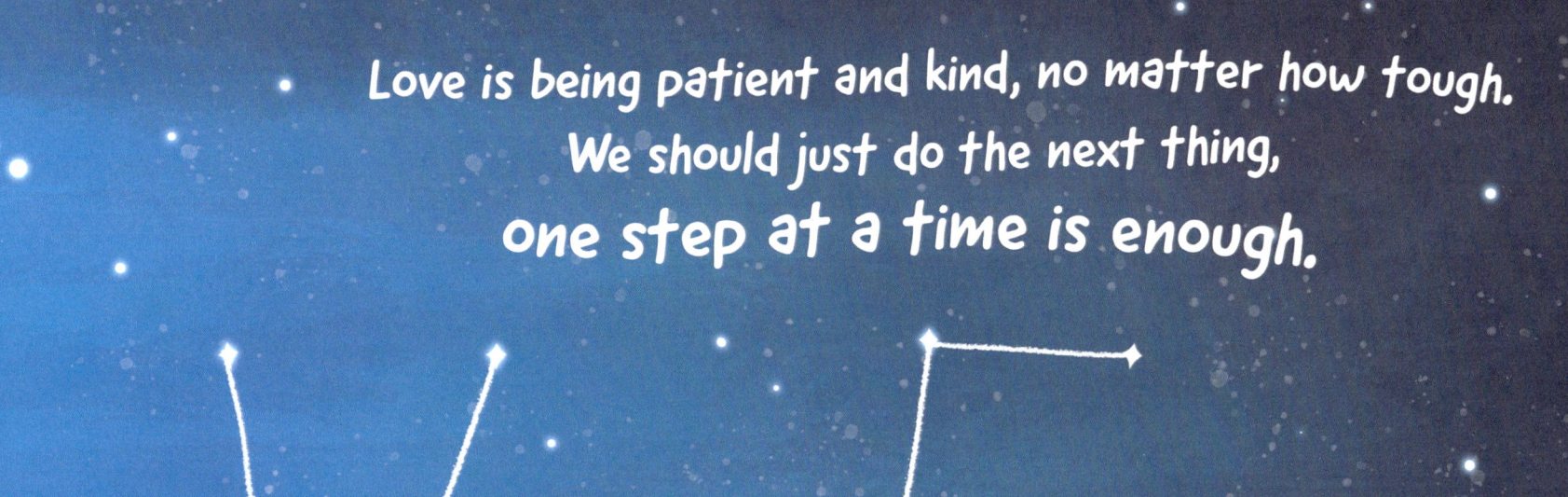

Now, as for you, little one,
is it time for your sleep?
Where will your little legs take you
as you drift off and dream?

Louie and Rascal

Spike

A big-paw thank you to my pals, Rascal and Spike,

for making our dream for this book come true!

Love, Louie!

The Louie Crew thanks you for taking the time to read this book. We're hard at work writing and designing the next few books in our series.

The Magic of Perseverance (with Noli Cannoli)
The Magic of Humility (with Daddy Long Legs)
The Magic of Joy (with Mr. McMurphy)
The Magic of Loyalty (with Buddy Bud)
The Magic of Goodness (with Mac and Harley)

Please connect with us through our website, Unleash-Love.com. There you will find the latest information about our upcoming books, how to contact us directly, and how to connect with our social media platforms. If you are a school or a nonprofit organization, please reach out to us for our special programs and donations to help children and schools eradicate bullying by loving others and being patient and kind.

CPSIA information can be obtained
at www.ICGtesting.com
Printed in the USA
LVRC101938051121
702555LV00002B/11